THE WOLFSONG SERIES

The WHISPERING STONES

SAVIOUR PIROTTA

ILLUSTRATED BY
DAVIDE ORTU

CONtENts

The JOURNEY

Great Island

Before the Beginning

Greetings from Great Island, as we who live here like to call it. It really is quite a huge island compared to the many others scattered like seashells in the sea around it. We have lakes and fertile land as far as the eye can see.

My name is Wolf. I am the youngest son of Bear, a farmer. For years, I considered myself the weaker son. My brother Hawk is stronger and cleverer than me. I, on the other hand, am a bit of a dreamer. I make silly mistakes, like going down to the shore for auk eggs when the tide is coming in, or falling asleep when I should be looking after the sheep.

And yet when a sacred spear was stolen from our burial mound, it was me who brought it back. I embarked on a great adventure with my dog, Shadow, to find it and I came back a changed person. Now I know what I want to be when I grow up. I want to be a healer and a shaman.

I made two great friends during my adventures too: Crow and Sparrow. Crow is the daughter of a chief and a fierce warrior. Sparrow is my spirit-brother. We made an agreement during my first adventure that we would be friends for life. Unfortunately, both Crow and Sparrow live on other islands, but I think of them every day.

I haven't yet told anyone in my village about wanting to become a healer. I reckon my father is not a great believer in the powers of the hidden world, although he pays his respects to the spirits every day. His is the rough world of farming and hunting. He believes in the power of the sharpened axe and the flying spear.

The rest of the village would probably laugh if I told them. Our people have huge respect for the shaman. Would they accept a weakling like me as their contact with the hidden world?

Chapter 1
The Return of the Spear

I went to see Moon, our shaman, the morning after I got home. Moon is the only person I could confide in. He has been kind to me all my life. He listened closely as I recounted my story, cocking his head to one side to hear better.

'You managed to draw the spear out of the corpse's hands when your friend could not. That proves you are favoured by the hidden world. Perhaps you will be much more powerful than I one day. You may help people in ways that I never could.

'But becoming a shaman and a healer is not so easy. There will be many tests. The forces of darkness will try to lead you astray. But I will be here to help you. I shall be your teacher and your guide.'

I felt almost embarrassed by these words of kindness.

'Thank you,' was all I could manage to say.

'But first we must return the stolen spear to its rightful owner, as soon as possible,' said the shaman. 'It's been missing too long already.'

We had to wait a good nine days before we could do that. A burial mound can only be opened on special days or the spirits will get angry. It was a cold night, and a stiff wind blew off the sea below our village. There was a light dusting of snow on the ground. Some people had brought torches, but they did not give much light.

'A new moon brings new beginnings,' the shaman explained, as the village gathered outside the burial mound. 'It's a time to right old wrongs, to make new promises and start new journeys. This will be a fresh start for our village. We can all go about our daily lives knowing we are protected again.'

Father and the village axe-maker opened the door to the burial mound. This was a huge flat stone that had to be dragged aside. Several people stepped back, as if scared that something dangerous might come crawling out of the darkness. Shadow growled. The shaman held the spear up for everyone to see. The thief had thrown away the wooden shaft so he could hide the spearhead better but the shaman had made a new one. This one too was decorated with leaping dolphins and deer, as well as flashes of lightning carved in thin strips. It was beautiful.

'Our protection from bad luck and disease had been stolen, but Wolf has brought it back,' he said loudly. 'I shall now return it to its rightful owner. Let this be the end of the matter. Let no one harbour any ill feeling towards Wolf and his family.'

I half-expected the people to cheer but there

was not a sound. As far as the village was concerned, I was no hero. I had been responsible for the theft of the spear, by letting a stranger into the village. Still, it was disappointing.

Moon signalled for his son, Rain, to hand me a torch. 'Wolf will come into the House of the Dead with me.'

'But Father,' protested Rain, shooting me a dark look. 'I am your son! It is my right to help you with your work.' In the light of the flaming torch, his eyes were pools of angry darkness.

'I said Wolf will come with me,' the shaman repeated firmly. 'This is his journey and he must see it to the end.'

Rain thrust the torch at me and I took it without looking him in the eye. I knew Moon was right. This was my journey. But I still felt guilty about causing bad blood between father and son. I followed Moon into a long passage. My father, the axe-maker and several others hurried on before us to push aside a second stone block. This led into a wider corridor.

'You men go outside and wait until I call you,' ordered the shaman, his voice echoing in the near-darkness. My father and his men retreated, leaving us alone. I held up the torch, which lit up the entrance of a chamber at the end of the passage. A warm, musty smell came from it. The floor was covered in skeletons, all laid out carefully on their side as if sleeping. Before my great adventure, I had been scared of human skulls and bones. Now they just filled me with respect for the ancestors who once lived among us, but whose spirits now dwelt in the hidden world.

'Make sure you don't trip over them,' warned the shaman, picking his way towards a small doorway on the side of the chamber. Beyond the doorway was a smaller room, with round walls. More skeletons were clustered around a wooden platform, on which lay the dead healer, his skull resting on a small pillow of yellowed cloth.

The first time I'd seen this skeleton, I had been too scared to look at it properly. Now all I could feel was a sense of peace washing over me. My adventure had indeed changed me.

'Step forward and give him back his spear,' said Moon gently. 'I shall sing to him and tell him how sorry we are that it was stolen. I shall promise that we will never let it happen again.'

'May I sing too?' I asked.

In truth, my song is more of a long drawn-out wolf howl. I had sung it once before, in a moment of great danger, and it had brought me help. Now I felt the urge to sing it again but for a different reason.

'I am sure that would please the spirit of the healer very much,' said the shaman.

I threw back my head and sang. I apologised to the healer for letting his spear be stolen, I assured him the crime would never happen again.

My song echoed around the burial mound. Then I stepped up to the healer with the spear. For a horrible moment, I thought his bony fingers might twitch as I placed the spear in their grasp. But they didn't move. Moon stepped forward to make sure I had done the job properly.

'Please keep on protecting our village,' I whispered to the ancient healer. 'We are helpless without you.'

As I spoke, I noticed the healer had an amulet tied to his throat. A long time ago it had lain on his chest, but now it dangled through the ribcage. The wind blew in from the passage and the amulet swung on the end of its string. Then the string broke and the precious object fell onto the platform. It rolled across the wooden slats and dropped at my feet.

I stared at it, wide-eyed.

'The ancient healer wants you to have it,' said Moon. 'It's a gift! He is marking you out as a friend. It means he will look out for you and protect you. It seems you are indeed to be a healer like him. Thank him... and accept it.'

Half-scared, half-excited, I reached out and gingerly picked up the amulet. It was a polished bird's skull, small and round like a pebble.

Later, lying in bed, I looked at it by the light of the fire. The bone skull glowed in my hands like a pearl. There was a little hole on either side of it where the ears had once been. Two tiny, dark pebbles filled up the eye sockets. They were painted to resemble eyes and, even now the colour had faded, they looked almost real. The beak was small and slightly curved. I wondered what kind of bird it had been.

Why had the dead healer given it to me? Had he really been creating a bond between us, like Moon had said? Did it possess some hidden power like the sacred spear?

CHAPTER 2
The Bird-Skull Amulet

As the days passed and the nights got longer, I almost forgot about the amulet hanging round my neck. Life went back to what it had been before my adventure. I might have had secret ambitions to become a healer, but I still had to help out on the farm and look after the flock.

It was freezing cold sitting out in the meadow but shepherding was the only time I had to unwind. The only time I could think and dream, although now I was careful not to fall asleep. I did not want to lose another lamb.

Rain still continued to harass me. He would often leap out at me when I least expected him to, making me jump.

'There goes the village traitor,' he would jeer.

I usually managed to ignore him, but on midwinter's day, shuffling through the newly-fallen snow to take over from Hawk at the meadow, I met him coming up the sea path. He had four other boys with him and a girl in black furs. I recognised two of the boys and the girl. She was the herb-gatherer's daughter. They were from our village, but the other two were strangers.

'There goes the traitor I told you about.' Rain nudged one of the boys I didn't recognise. 'He looks like a helpless shepherd but, believe me, he's got this village into *big* trouble. He let a complete stranger in and she robbed us.'

That was a bit rich seeing as Rain was talking to a stranger himself. Still, I had learnt not to take his bait.

'Your father said we must put the past behind us,' I said calmly. 'The stolen spear is back where it belongs. No harm done.'

'But for how long?' growled Rain. 'I bet you are secretly hoping your thieving little friend from across the sea will come and see you soon. Won't she be tempted to break into the burial mound again and steal something else?'

The 'little friend' Rain was referring to was, of course, Crow. She wasn't little though. In fact, she was even taller than Rain. And stronger, which probably made him feel insecure.

'You're just jealous because she towers over you,' I said. 'She could beat you in a fight any day.'

There was a ripple of laughter from Rain's friends but I couldn't tell if they were sneering at me or him. Rain spat at my feet.

'A girl beat me in a fight? Never, shepherd-boy. Hurry along and don't fall asleep on the job again today, or your family will soon have no flock left. Come on.' He gestured to his friends. 'Let's try and get to the hunting grounds before the sun is fully up. I'm going to catch a deer today.

We'll roast it over at my place and have ourselves a proper midwinter feast.'

But talking about Crow reminded me about the only part of the mystery I still had to solve.

'Those blue beads you claimed to have found outside the entrance to the burial mound,' I called after Rain. He stopped in his tracks, looking over his shoulder. 'The ones you used to convince everyone that Crow had stolen the spear,' I continued. 'Did you really find them there or did you get them from somewhere else, just to get me into trouble?'

Rain grinned from ear to ear. 'Wouldn't you like to know, dreamer-boy?'

I stood there fuming as he sauntered away with his friends, the snow crunching under their feet. Shadow barked after them.

'Let's not waste time being angry at those fools,' I said to Shadow. He trotted after me as I began walking again. It started to snow lightly and I wondered if it would last until night-time.

Midwinter is the longest night of the year. We have a special celebration to mark the middle of winter. From today on, the nights will get shorter. Soon it will be spring and the earth will wake up again to fill our lives with warmth and greenery, and fresh food.

They say that a snowfall during the midwinter celebration is a sign that the spirits are happy, and that we are going to make it safely through the dark and hostile winter. I met a few farmers hurrying home with a sheep in tow. It made me think of the feast to come and my tummy rumbled with hunger.

When I got home, neighbours were gathering at our house. Mother had roasted one of our own sheep for the occasion, and made a dipping sauce for it with dried herbs and fat. The feasting lasted long into the night and the sound of laughter and singing echoed along the covered passages that connect all the houses in the village. At last, our bellies full to bursting with food and drink, we left the warmth of our fireplaces and gathered outside the burial mound.

A light snow was still falling.

'Welcome,' said the shaman, who'd been waiting for us. 'I hope you have all enjoyed your feasts, and that your laughter was loud enough to be heard by the spirits. They take great pleasure in knowing you enjoy the benefits of their kindness. And now we must honour our dead ancestors, so that they might speak on our behalf with the stars and the spirits. They shall remind the sleeping earth that it will soon be time to wake up again, to bring forth springtime.'

Once again, my father and the axe maker moved aside the burial mound's stone door, revealing the dark passage inside. The sun was about to rise and the seagulls wheeled around in the air, cawing loudly. Far below the village, huge waves crashed against the shore. I could feel a mysterious power in the air, as if invisible spirits were gathering round too.

'Hear us, oh fathers and mothers long gone,' called out Moon. 'We share with you the first light of a new dawn, so you might feel its warmth once again. Know that we remember and respect you, and that we seek your protection from the dark and the dangerous.'

As Moon spoke, the first rays of the sun shone across the sky. The sea and the snow-covered land glowed a warm pink and the birds took to the air in great, swooping clouds. I watched in awe as the sun reached through the open doors of the burial mound to fill the passage and the great chamber with bright light.

I thought of the dead healer lying on his wooden platform, the healing spear clutched in his bony fingers, and my hand went to the strange amulet at my throat. Suddenly it twitched between my fingers, making me jump.

I glanced around to see if anyone was looking. No one was giving me the slightest bit of notice because the shaman was playing his flute and the sun's rays were moving across the burial mound. I risked a look at the amulet. Was it my imagination or were the stone eyes much brighter than usual, the pupils a shiny jet black? They seemed to be looking directly at me.

As soon as the shaman dismissed the crowd, I set off to the meadow. My head was in a spin. I kept taking the amulet out from under my tunic and looking at it again. The eyes were still shining. What did that mean? Had the healer's spirit reached out of the burial mound and awakened some kind of power inside it?

Hawk was waiting impatiently outside the shepherd's hut. 'Is there any roast meat left from the feast?' he asked. Even on such an important night, my father had refused to let him take time off from his shepherding. Family duties always came first.

'Aye, Mother left you plenty. And ale too.'

Hawk grinned. 'Good. I'm famished.'

He disappeared down the path faster than a

hare. I made sure the sheep were all safe. Some of them were carrying babies, so losing one of them would get me into twice the trouble. Then I settled down outside the hut and held the amulet in the palm of my hand. Shadow sniffed at it and growled very softly. But he didn't try to lick it as he did with most things. The eyes were still shining.

'What do you think made it twitch, Shadow?' I asked. 'And what am I supposed to do next? Am I supposed to use it in some way? But what for? And how?'

Shadow had no answers and neither did I.

The amulet was a complete mystery.

Chapter 3
Dreaming of Snakes

That night I couldn't go to sleep. I tossed and turned all night, while my parents snored with their faces to the wall. I held up the amulet and looked at it again. In the light of the dying fire, the eyes shone even brighter. They almost seemed to be smiling.

'What am I meant to do with you?' I begged. 'Please, tell me…'

Suddenly the amulet started swinging back and forth on its string. I stared at it dumbfounded. It was doing this on its own, with no help from me. The stone eyes stayed fixed into mine. They seemed to get bigger and bigger, blotting out the room, drawing me into their shiny, inky darkness. I felt dizzy, my head spun, then the darkness swallowed me up and I fell headlong into it…

…I landed with a thump on a sandy floor. The amulet was still dangling from my neck. Scrabbling to my feet, I peered around. I knew right away I was not on Great Island anymore. Everything around me felt strange, unreal. As my eyes got used to the near-dark, I could see I was in a cave. I made out a vast wilderness outside. Lightning kept flashing across the sky in great jagged streaks. The land looked rocky and barren. It was littered with the bones of long-dead animals, which I could see as clearly as if I was standing next to them.

Strangely, I could hear nothing, only see. I noticed a small fire burning under a cooking pot. A dark shape appeared at the mouth of the cave and came towards it. It was someone wrapped in thick furs. Their face was covered by a hood and they carried a shepherd's stick with a hook at one end.

A small flock of sheep lumbered in after them. Perhaps this cave was their shelter during a storm. The shepherd stirred the pot with the end of their stick, poked the fire and lay down to rest on the sandy ground. The sheep settled all around.

An icy wind blew into the cave, nearly blowing out the fire. The shepherd jumped up at once and grabbed a bundle of twigs, thrusting them under the pot. Bright orange flames flared up around it, making the stew inside overflow. Without warning, a long, black shadow streaked out of the burning wood, straight and fast as an arrow.

It was a snake with bared fangs, and it was aiming at the shepherd's throat.

The shepherd fell back, hands clutching at their throat, and that's when a sound pierced the silent dream. The shepherd screamed...

...and I sat up, a silent scream of my own stuck deep in my chest. My hair was plastered to my head with sweat. Shadow whined softly and nuzzled against me. I was back in my own bed, the straw from my mattress scattered all over the floor. The bird skull amulet was still around my neck. I looked at it closely. The stone eyes had gone dull but the beak was open in a strange smile.

'Wolf, is anything the matter? I thought I heard Shadow growl.' My mother sat up on one elbow, squinting at me from across the room. The house always gets filled with smoke from the dying fire towards morning, making it difficult to see. I was glad about that.

'I'm fine,' I said, quickly stuffing the amulet inside my tunic. 'I just had a bad dream.'

'Get some water,' said Mother. 'But quietly. Don't wake up your father. He has a busy day ahead. And try to go back to sleep yourself. It's nearly dawn.'

I fetched some water from the stone trough in the corner and lay back on my furry blanket.

But I couldn't go back to sleep, no matter how hard I tried. I was sure the amulet had caused my dream. It had sent me a warning. Someone was in danger of being bitten by a deadly snake. Someone who was a shepherd—someone like my brother Hawk.

ChapteR 4
The Meaning of Dreams

I slipped out the door the moment I heard my mother snoring again, Shadow squeezing through behind me. I don't know how I managed it. Front doors in our village are made of thick stone and really heavy to push aside.

I pleaded with the spirits as I ducked out of the tunnel leading to our house. 'Please, don't let my dream have come true yet. Let Hawk be safe.'

The ground was slippery with ice but I didn't stop running until I reached the meadow. The door to the little shepherd's hut was shut against the cold but I could see the glow of a fire through the tiny window. Hawk was whistling inside. What a relief! He was still alive.

'Don't throw any more sticks on the fire!' I shouted, tearing the door open. 'There might be a snake lurking in them.'

'Good morning, little brother,' said Hawk, holding up his hands. 'You're up early today.'

'I mean what I said,' I blurted. 'Don't throw wood on the fire without checking it first. I had a dream about it. You were sheltering from a storm in a cave, and when you threw a bundle of twigs on the fire, a snake leapt out. It got you in the throat.'

'But I never go into caves to shelter from the rain,' said Hawk, confused. 'I just sit in this hut.'

I frowned. 'I have to admit the cave did seem a bit strange. But I still think you should be careful.'

'I'm not afraid of snakes,' said Hawk, 'but thanks for the warning. I'll look through the firewood very carefully from now on.'

'Promise?' I insisted.

'I promise,' laughed Hawk. 'You are a good brother, Wolf. Now I'd better get going seeing as you're already here. I could help Mother make the breakfast porridge.'

Once Hawk had left, I took out the amulet and thanked the spirit of the dead healer. The warning dream might have just saved my brother's life.

Moon nodded gravely when I told him about the amulet later that day.

'It must be a dream amulet,' he said. 'Touching the sacred spear brought you visions. But the ancient healer knows you can't carry that around with you. So he gave you his amulet instead. It is sending you seeing-dreams. But you must be very careful. The power is strong inside you, Wolf, but it is not easy to read dreams. Some things you see in the dreams brought on by the amulet will have hidden meanings. They are *symbols*. You must learn to find out what they are really trying to tell you.'

I thought about Moon's words for a few moments. 'You mean if I see an eagle in a special dream it might not be an eagle at all but a symbol for something else?'

'That is exactly what I mean,' replied Moon. 'An eagle is a powerful creature. Its wings can take it to the top of mountains. When you see an eagle in a dream, it might be a symbol for someone powerful and daring enough to climb a mountain, like a village chief or a famous hunter.'

'I see,' I said, although I did not like the idea of symbols at all—surely it wasn't that hard? My dream had been pretty clear and simple, and I'd guessed its meaning at once. 'So in my dream I saw a…'

But Moon put a finger to his lips and stopped me. 'Shush! You must never reveal what you see in your seeing-dreams except to the person they are intended to help. You have a long road ahead of you, Wolf. Understanding seeing-dreams is one of the most difficult tasks a shaman can do. It will take a long time to master the skill. You must ask the spirits to help you, as I myself have never had the gift of seeing-dreams.'

'But the spirits have shown you new hunting grounds,' I said.

'True,' said the shaman, 'but those were rare gifts sent after much sacrifice. They were just fleeting images of places where our hunters can find fresh prey, mere pictures compared to the complex seeing-dreams you have been granted. Studying the meaning of the symbols in seeing-dreams can take years. Proceed carefully—if you get the meaning of a dream wrong, there could be fatal consequences...'

'For me?' I asked.

'For the person you're meant to help.'

For the first time in my life, I found myself disagreeing with Moon. I found the idea of symbols confusing. If the spirits wanted to help you, why would they send you a warning you might not understand? Why didn't they just send a simple message you could read immediately, so you could act right away? No, I was sure that's what the spirits had done in my seeing-dream. They'd shown me my brother Hawk getting bitten by a snake. And the warning had saved his life.

As I walked home, I felt very proud of myself. I had taken a giant step closer to becoming a shaman. Once I'd had a few more seeing-dreams and helped a few people with my warnings, my reputation would grow in the village.

Then people like Rain and his band of tough friends would have to stop putting me down and show me some respect.

Chapter 5
Wolf Moon

Although I stared at it long and hard, willing the eyes to start shining again, the amulet refused to bring me any more seeing-dreams. Impatient, I turned to the spirits for help, leaving little sacrifices of leaves and nuts at the feet of ancient rocks.

They refused to help me, and no dreams came.

For a few days after midwinter, the sun shone from a cloudless sky, which filled the village and the countryside with a weak light. Then the sky darkened again and the snow returned. It seemed as if the winter would never come to an end.

One afternoon, the shaman came out to the

meadow to see me. I had taken shelter from the cold in the shepherd's hut, bringing the sheep in with me. They did not mind the cold but their hooves often rotted from standing too long in the wet snow.

Shadow growled softly and wagged his tail as Moon ducked to clear the low doorway.

'Good day,' he said. 'Are you well?'

'Yes, thank you,' I said politely. I knew that Moon was a very busy man and that this visit meant he had something important to tell me. I sat up. 'I'm afraid I've already eaten my lunch. I have nothing to offer you.'

'Don't worry about that.' Moon sat on the floor with some difficulty. He fiddled with the knot on a bundle he'd brought with him. 'I have observed you going about the village, and I know you are disappointed that the amulet has not sent you any more dreams. So I have made you a little gift, to lift your spirits. Here, I made it myself.'

He handed me a clay bowl. It was beautifully

decorated with wolves following each other round the rim.

I had to try very hard to stop my voice from cracking. No one outside my family had ever given me a gift before. 'Thank you! I shall treasure it always,' I whispered.

'When you become a shaman, you will have a lot of uses for this bowl. You will drink from it during rituals.'

I admired the paintings and traced my finger

along them. 'The wolves are beautiful.'

'Speaking of wolves,' said Moon, 'it is the time of the Wolf Moon.'

'Yes,' I nodded.

Indeed, the moon was turning red like blood already. It was the time when wolves howled louder and longer than usual. They sang to the hidden spirits so that they may protect their cubs and help them survive the last of the cold winter.

'The Wolf Moon is a time of powerful magic,' said Moon. 'Wolves have the spirits of warriors. They are cunning and fearless. I am attending a secret shaman ceremony in honour of them, where I shall make a sacrifice to the wolves so that they might fill my own spirit with their courage. Seeing as you are named after the wolf, and that you will be a shaman yourself one day, I thought you might like to come with me? There will be other shamans there. You will not be allowed to take part in the sacrifice, but you can watch. It will be good for you to see how shamans work with one another, and perhaps you can ask the wolves in your own way to make you bolder too.'

I shot to my feet in excitement. 'I would love to come very much! But if it's a secret ceremony, will the other shamans let me watch?'

Moon nodded. 'Aye, we sometimes let young men who have already started on the path of becoming shamans attend our ceremonies. It doesn't happen very often, mind.' He got slowly to his feet. 'I have already spoken to your father and he has given his permission.'

'You spoke to my father?' I gasped.

'Don't worry,' laughed Moon. 'I haven't told him you want to be a shaman. That is for you to reveal when the time comes. I merely told him I am going on a short journey and that I needed a companion, someone who can carry my goatskin.'

'Thank the spirits,' I laughed. 'I will tell my father when I am ready. Did you hear that, Shadow? I am going to attend a secret ceremony.' Shadow barked.

'It is settled then,' said Moon. 'Meet me tonight at moonrise by the great stone that marks the entrance to our village. Make sure you wear all your warm furs. It'll be extremely cold. It's best to leave Shadow. He might find the ritual frightening.'

I felt sad at the thought of leaving Shadow behind. He was always by my side, but I trusted Moon's reasoning. When he left, I stuck my head out of the window to see if it was getting dark yet. It wasn't. Despite the whirling snow, the afternoon was still bright. I had a long time to wait before Hawk came to take my place in the meadow.

I tried to pass the time by staring at the amulet, willing it to send me another dream. When that didn't work, I braved the cold to gather twigs and sticks for the fire. Hawk would be pleased to see a big woodpile when he arrived.

Then, after making sure all the sheep were safely inside with me, I curled up in a corner of the hut and went to sleep.

Hawk shook me awake what seemed a few moments later. In fact, it was after sunset. I washed my face in the snow outside, hurried home to wolf down my evening meal and, after leaving a very disappointed Shadow with Mother, I raced to meet Moon by the great stone.

It had stopped snowing and a large moon had come up. It hung low in the sky, glowing a bright red as if it were filled with blood. I could see bats dancing against it. It was a spooky sight.

The snow on the ground glowed a pale pink in the strange moonlight. My breath formed little clouds in the air and I was glad of my thick furs. My mother had packed some deer meat and barley cakes for the journey. I clutched the bag tightly, comforted by the thought that the food would keep us alive if we got lost in a sudden snowstorm. I had my new bowl with me too. From now on, I was planning to take it everywhere with me. Not only was it proof that I could one day be a shaman, it was a reminder that someone actually respected me.

Moon arrived with a bundle over one shoulder. He had a spear tied to his back, but not for hunting, he explained. It was needed for the ceremony.

A hulking shape followed him, kicking up snow. I knew who it was even before it opened its mouth to speak and my heart sank. Rain!

'Father,' he said, ignoring me completely, 'I know you're going to a secret ceremony. I saw you getting ready. I demand you take me with you. It is my right as your son.'

'Go back home, Rain,' replied Moon patiently. 'I've told you many times, this is not your fate. I do not have time to argue right now. Make sure the fire in the hearth doesn't go out.'

Rain glared in my direction. 'You think he'll make a better shaman than me. But you're wrong! He's just a weakling. I am cleverer than he is, and stronger!'

The shaman spoke through gritted teeth.

49

'Being a shaman isn't about being clever or tough, Rain. It's about helping people, whether you like them or not. It's about listening and acting with your heart, guided by your spirit, not hitting out with your fists. Things that you constantly fail to do. The spirits have chosen Wolf, and I for one think they have made the right choice.'

Moon turned and started walking away. Rain's face burned from his father's words and he turned his furious eyes to me. They were narrow slits, full of hatred.

'You'll be sorry you made an enemy out of me, wolf-boy,' Rain growled at me as his friends slipped out from behind the rocks to join him. 'You have no idea who you're messing with.'

Rain's friends sniggered and a few spat in my direction. The sound made my skin crawl. Without another word, I hurried to catch up with Moon.

We walked for quite some time, while the Wolf Moon rose high in the sky. A thick mist formed, wrapping us up in a fleecy dampness. It was hard to see through it, not that I think we passed anything much to see. There was no glimmer of light to indicate a village or a lonely farm. It was strangely silent.

At last we came to a wide, fast flowing stream with large stepping stones across it. On the other bank, I could see glowing eyes in the bushes, staring and blinking. It was a pack of silent wolves, watching and waiting. I turned to Moon, suddenly afraid, but he only smiled.

'Do not be afraid. They are the guardians of the wild lands we are entering. They have come to show us the way to the secret meeting place, and to make sure we respect the land. We must not take anything we find on the other side of the stream. Everything there belongs only to the spirits.'

Although I am proud to be named after the wolf, and still believe that wolves protect me, I had never been so close to a whole pack before. These wolves were huge, with pointed yellow teeth and quivering snouts. My heart was beating loudly enough to burst as I slowly picked my way across the slippery stepping stones.

'Wolf, let me lean on your shoulder,' said Moon. 'I am not as steady on my feet as I used to be.'

He reached out to me and the bag slipped off his shoulder to be carried away by the current.

'My drinking bowl,' gasped Moon, 'and my best flint knife. I was going to offer it as sacrifice.'

'Shall I go after them?' I said.

'No,' sighed Moon, with one last look at the fast disappearing bag, 'it's too dangerous. And we'll be late.'

The wolves surged in the mist as we reached the bank. Moon and I stopped for a moment to regain our breath then climbed a hill, very much like a burial mound, but with a massive, ancient tree on top.

Our island is not known for its trees. The wind is too fierce to allow anything

higher than a prickly bush to grow. But here, on the crest of this hill, was a tree bigger and taller than any I'd seen on my journeys. Its branches reached out through the mist and I could see round, shiny objects dangling from them. They jangled against each other, making an eerie sound.

'It is a sacred oak,' said Moon. 'It is believed the spirits sent the acorn to our island long before people came to live here. Its roots grow deep into the earth, holding it together. There are rumours that if it is ever chopped down, the entire world will crumble to dust. Those things dangling from the branches are amulets. Some have been left by the shamans who arrived for the secret ceremony before us. Healers leave pouches of sacred herbs too, so that the magic of the tree will make them stronger. I had an amulet of my own to hang up in both our names, but the stream took it. I hope the spirit of the oak will not be offended if we walk past it without leaving a token of our respect. Come, Wolf...'

We both bowed at the tree as we passed, and Moon chanted some kind of spell. On the other side of the hill was a narrow valley, running like a deep, jagged scar in the earth. Moon and I hurried along it until we saw a light ahead, shining high up through the mist.

'We are nearly there,' breathed Moon.

We clambered up the rocks to discover the light was in the mouth of a cave. A group of men, their faces hidden under large fur hoods, stood waiting.

'Welcome, old friend,' they said to Moon, reaching out to help him into the cave. 'And who is our young guest?'

'His name is Wolf,' answered the shaman. 'I think the spirits have chosen him to be one of us when he is older. It would be good for him to watch tonight's ceremony.'

'Welcome, young Wolf,' said one of the shamans. 'With a name like that, you should find our ritual fascinating. My name is Elk. I shall be the leader of our group tonight, the master of ceremonies.'

'I am honoured to be here, with such important people,' I replied.

Elk led us deeper into the cave where a huge fire was burning. The shamans all removed their cloaks and formed a circle around it, while I found a corner where I could watch.

Elk called, 'We are all gathered here to pay our respects to the spirit of the wolf.'

'Hear! Spirits hear!' chanted the shamans. 'The spirit of

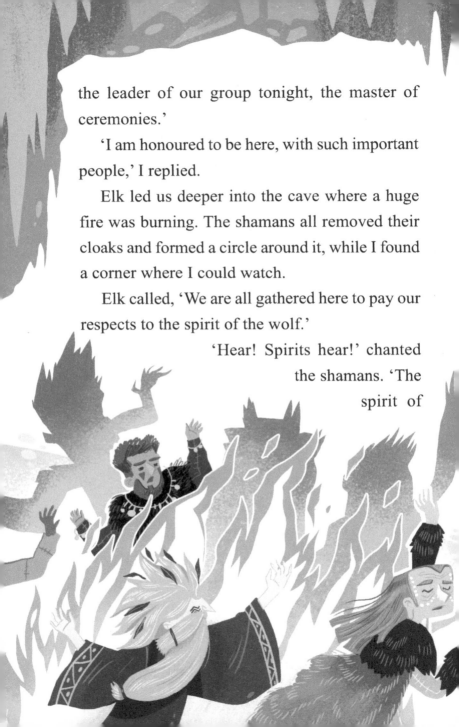

the wolf is indeed the most powerful.'

'We offer sacrifice,' shouted Elk. He placed an arrow, a spear and a knife onto the fire. 'Behold, these are the weapons that kill the wolf. We swear never to use them.'

'We swear never to use violence against the wolves,' repeated the shamans, and they all stepped forward to fling their own weapons into the fire, including Moon who still had his spear.

'In return, we ask you to fill our own spirits with your courage and your cunning,' cried Elk.

'Your courage and your cunning,' echoed the shamans.

They threw back their heads and howled like wolves. The noise was echoed outside; our wolf guides had joined in the ritual. The howling bounced off the cave walls. The smoke from the sacrifice stung

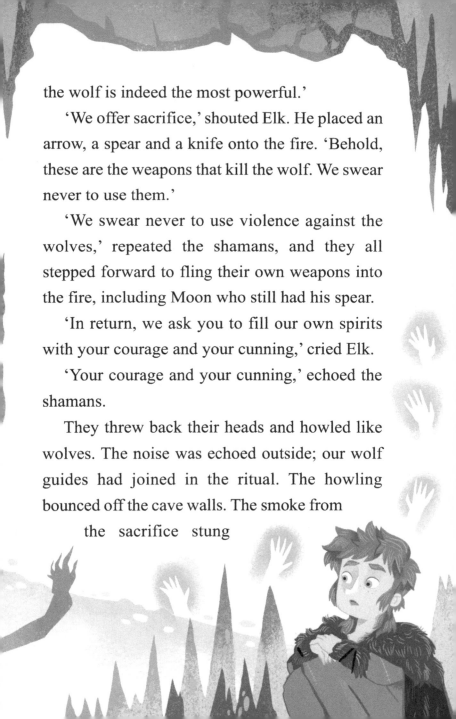

my eyes while the shamans started dancing round the fire.

My heart beat wildly in my chest as I watched them, my feet itching to join in. I don't know how long I sat there, but at last the fire started to die down, leaving no trace of the sacrificed weapons. It was as if they had disappeared by magic. Outside, the sky was growing lighter. The shamans all fell to the floor, exhausted and drenched in sweat.

Elk fetched a bulging goatskin. 'We must all drink,' he said. 'To clean our minds and revive our spirits. Come, I have clean water.'

Some of the men got up to fetch drinking bowls.

'I have nothing to drink out of,' murmured Moon, his breath still short from the dancing. 'I lost my drinking bowl in the stream. I will have to borrow one after the others have finished.'

'No need,' I said, opening my bundle. 'I brought your gift with me. Here, you can be the first to use it.' I held out the bowl so Elk could fill it with water.

Moon gulped from it greedily. 'I do believe water is the most precious gift the spirits have given us.' He had barely finished his words when his eyes bulged and his hands clawed at his throat, as if trying to tear something out of it. The other shamans and I stared in horror as Moon fell sideways and my bowl shattered on the ground.

Elk rushed over. 'His lips have turned dark,' he cried. 'His throat is swelling. He's been poisoned!'

CHAPTER 6
Wolfsbane and Mustard Seeds

I stood rooted to the spot with terror. Elk turned to the other shamans who quickly gathered round. 'We must act quickly if we are to save Moon's life. His breathing is very weak.'

He spoke to a very old man with a wrinkled face and bushy eyebrows. 'Moss, you are the healer with the most experience here. What are we to do?'

'Lay him on his stomach,' replied Moss, reaching for one of the larger shards of my bowl which had come to rest against the wall. He turned it round slowly in his gnarled hands and sniffed at the inside.

'Our friend has been poisoned with a herb called Wolfsbane,' he said.

'But if the poison was in the water, why did it affect only Moon?' asked one of the other shaman. 'We all drank.'

'The poison must have been in the bowl,' said Moss.

The shamans all turned to me and I felt the blood drain from my face.

'I would never hurt Moon,' I defended myself. 'He is my mentor.'

'We haven't got much time,' said Elk. 'Please, Moss, what are we to do?'

The old healer closed his eyes to concentrate. 'We need mustard seeds. I shall make a potion with them. They are known for healing a person who's swallowed Wolfsbane. But we have not much time. Does anyone here have any mustard seeds?'

All the shamans looked from one to another.

'I left some as an offering at the Sacred Oak

many moons ago,' said one of them who I knew was called Talon. 'I shall go and fetch them.'

'There is not enough time for you to go,' interrupted Elk. 'Your aged knees will slow you down. Let Wolf fetch them. He will be much faster.'

'But it's still unclear whether he poisoned Moon,' argued Talon, and some of the others nodded to show they agreed with him.

'We'll have to take that chance,' snapped Elk. 'We have no choice, Moon is on the verge of dying.' He turned to me. 'Run like the wind and come back with the seeds, or the spirits will haunt you forever.'

'You will recognise my pouch by the image of a bull I stitched on it,' said Talon. 'It is high up in

the tree, almost at the top.'

'The spirits of the wolves go with you!' called Elk, as I scrambled out of the cave and down the rocks to the bottom of the valley.

I don't think I've ever run so fast in my life. Without thinking, I hopped over stones and stumbled through prickly bushes, which slashed my tunic and leggings.

All the while, I was aware of the wolves running alongside me. To be honest, I wasn't sure if they were really there or just in my imagination, but I was glad of their presence just the same. The blood red moon looked down at me from the misty sky and I howled my Wolf Song at it, begging it to let me get to the sacred tree and back in time to save Moon's life.

I got to the oak, panting and gasping for breath. Praying to the spirits to give me strength, I hauled myself up into the branches, searching for the leather pouch with the bull symbol. I found it hidden among the jangling amulets and my hands yanked it off the branch. Stuffing it deep into my pocket, I leapt to the ground.

'Thank you,' I said to the oak. 'I shall come back with a thank you offering one day.'

I don't know how long it took me to get back but it was almost light when the shamans' hands reached out to haul me back into the cave.

'Is he still living?' I gasped, looking at Moon.

Elk nodded. 'Just about.'

Moss took the pouch from me and opened it calmly. The mustard seeds tumbled into his gnarled hand. He put them carefully onto a flat stone and I watched as he crushed them into a powder. This he put into a cup and mixed with water to form a potion, all the while whispering spells under his breath. The other shamans gathered round, laying their hands on Moon. Their voices united in a strange, chilling song as they asked the spirits for help.

Carefully, Elk poured the mustard seed potion into Moon's mouth. Moon shuddered, then a loud burp escaped his lips.

'He will survive,' whispered Moss, sounding relieved.

While I'd been fetching the mustard seeds, the shamans had tied a cloak between two branches to make a cot. They lifted Moon onto it and carried him out of the cave. He was shaking like a leaf by the time we reached his house. I was about to knock on the door when it opened and Rain came out.

'What do you want, wolf-boy?' he snapped. Then he saw the other shamans carrying Moon.

'Your father was poisoned but he survived,'

I replied weakly.

'Moss and Wolf saved his life,' said Elk. 'Let us in, young Rain. We need to take your father indoors this very moment. He has to be kept cool with cold water on his face and hands. He will be fine but he needs a lot of rest.'

I was about to follow the shamans inside but Rain stepped in my path. 'Not you. *You're* not welcome in our house. These doddery old men might think you helped save my father's life, but if he was poisoned there is only one person who had a reason to do it. *You.* You are so desperate to take his place that you would even stoop to murder. Just wait until I tell everyone. You will be banished from the village forever.'

ChapteR 7
A Hiding Place

A cloud of despair wrapped me in its dark embrace. Rain's words echoed in my head as I slipped away home. *You will be banished from the village forever.*

It was unfair. I had helped save Moon's life, not tried to kill him. I had no idea how the poison had got into the bowl but it must have been an accident.

It didn't take long for the news to spread around the village. Even as Mother was ladling out the breakfast, I could hear an angry crowd gathering in the passageway outside the house.

'Hold on to Shadow,' Father whispered to me.

'Make sure he doesn't bark.'

He opened the door, but only a crack so no one could peek in.

'Good morning,' he said. 'What brings so many of you to my door this early in the morning?'

'We heard your son tried to poison the shaman, Bear,' someone replied. It was the axe-maker's wife.

'That boy is a thorn in our side,' added someone else. 'First the stolen spear and now this. He needs to be punished. If you're too soft on the lad, one of us will do it for you.'

'You shouldn't believe everything you hear,' replied Father sternly.

'My son is no murderer. I'd let him explain everything himself but... he hasn't come home yet. Now, if you'll excuse me, my wife and I are about to have breakfast.'

He rammed the door shut but someone banged on it angrily. A child's voice shouted out.

'Next time you see Wolf, tell him we're going to get him.'

'That's Primrose, the herb-gatherer's daughter,' said Mother. 'She obviously isn't as gentle as her namesake. She should be helping her family, not wasting time outside our door making threats.'

'I saw her with Rain yesterday,' I said. 'She's one of his friends.'

We ate the porridge although, to be honest, I had no appetite. When we'd finished, Father said, 'It's dangerous for you to stay here, Wolf.

You must lie low until the shaman is strong enough to speak. Then, I have no doubt, he'll explain everything and clear your name. Meanwhile I know a good hiding place where no one will find you. I will take you there tonight, under the cover of darkness. For now, I'll go to the meadow and take over from Hawk.'

I was really glad neither of my parents had even asked if I'd committed the awful crime. I don't know what I would have done if they'd suspected I was guilty. The day passed very slowly, I tried weaving a basket but really, I was only listening out for the murmur of a crowd outside the door. Hawk slept for a while, then went out to meet his friends and returned for dinner. We ate in silence.

After what seemed like a lifetime, Father came back for his share of the evening meal. 'Everyone in the village will be asleep by now,' he said when he'd finished. 'Come on, Wolf. It's time to go. Keep Shadow close to you and make sure he doesn't bark. And pull your hood up. We mustn't be recognised.'

Mother handed me a bundle of food, while I made sure I had my flint knife and hard stones for making fire. I also checked my amulet was secure under my tunic.

After a quick hug from Mother, Father and I slipped out the door and along the covered passageways. A moment later, we were out of the village, with the cold wind blowing in our faces. Shadow stayed close to me.

'Where are we going, Father?' I said when the village was safely behind us. We had taken the road that led away from the sea and towards the freshwater lake where the village caught fish in the summer. It was frozen over now.

'There's an ancient hideout I discovered when I was your age,' replied Father, stopping near a huge rounded stone to let me catch up with him. 'People used it back in the days when marauders attacked our village on a regular basis. It was forgotten a long time ago, until I stumbled across it while chasing a deer. I never told anyone about it. It was my special hiding place when my father and mother got angry with me for not doing my chores properly, or when I just wanted to get away from everyone. It'll be a good hiding place for you.'

It had never occurred to me that my father could have disappointed his parents too when he was my age. 'What did you do to make your father angry?' I asked.

He chuckled. 'I hated looking for auk's eggs, and I would never collect dung for the fire. The smell made me throw up.'

We walked quickly across the frozen lake, poor Shadow's paws skittering on the ice, until we came to a small island roughly in the centre of the lake. It was covered in boulders, all leaning sideways as if half-sunk in the ground. Crows were perched on them and they cawed at us angrily. Even in the bright moonlight, this place looked like something out of a nightmare. Little wonder no one ever came here.

'How did that deer you were chasing get here?' I asked Father. 'Did it swim? Or was it winter, like now?'

'It was spring,' said Father. 'And I swam after it. I didn't catch it, mind. It was too fast for me. All I caught was a chill—I had to stay in bed for days.'

Behind one of the boulders was the smallest hut I'd ever seen, with a low entrance and no windows.

'How many people used to hide here at a time?' I asked Father.

'I should imagine ten, perhaps even twelve people used to squeeze in at a time,' he replied. 'And they would often stay for days, until they were absolutely sure the marauders were gone.'

I looked at the hut in horror. 'It's hard to believe all those people could fit in here.'

Father led the way in. 'That would have been

an entire village in those days. An extended family really.'

The hut had a low roof festooned with thick, dusty cobwebs. There wasn't even enough room to stand up. Shadow growled at a large spider, which scrambled away and hid in a crevice. I shuddered. How many other hairy monsters were lurking in the dark?

'Make yourself comfortable,' Father chuckled. It was the first time in many moons I'd heard him tell a joke. 'I know it's cramped but at least you'll be safe, son. Hawk will leave you food at the edge of the lake. He'll hide it behind that enormous round rock where we stopped. Make sure you check there is no one around if you light a fire. The listing boulders should hide you from anyone's view but you never know. And never light it outside, or at night. People will see that across the lake. I have no doubt Moon will soon come round and be able to talk. He'll clear your name, you'll see.'

He tousled my hair and left. Outside, the crows cawed angrily again as he made his way through the leaning boulders. But when he was gone, even they fell silent. For the first time in my life I actually missed Father. I wished he would stay, to protect me from the people in the village should they find me.

I fetched a stick from outside to clear away the cobwebs. Shadow, who thought we were going to have a game of throw-and-fetch, barked happily. 'Shush,' I said. 'It's the middle of the night. Some hunter on the shore might hear you.'

Once I'd got rid of the disgusting cobwebs, I sat down with my back to the wall. Shadow settled down with his nose on my knee. I tried eating some of the food Mother had packed but I still had no appetite. Instead I lit a fire. Now that I was alone, I had time to think. I felt really disappointed with the amulet. It had warned me about Hawk getting attacked by the snake. Why hadn't it sent me another dream about Moon?

Then it hit me. The amulet *had* tried to warn me. That dream I had wasn't about Hawk. It was about Moon. What was the shaman if not a shepherd whose work was to protect his people? I bet the snake was a just symbol too, an image for 'poison'.

Now I could see everything so clearly. The dream had warned me that Moon would be poisoned. Only, I had got it all wrong. I had not read the symbols properly. What had Moon said?

'Some things you see in the dreams brought on by the amulet will have hidden meanings. They are symbols. You must learn to find out what they are trying to tell you.'

But I had ignored his advice and acted hastily. My mistake had almost cost him his life. The amulet hadn't let me down. I had let myself down.

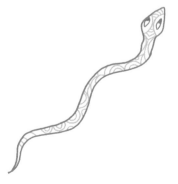

Chapter 8
A Daring Plan

I tried to push that horrible thought out of my mind but it wouldn't go away. It kept niggling away at me, keeping me awake for the rest of the night. When it got light, I went outside for a breath of fresh air. The sky was grey. It was going to be another cold day. The crows fixed their beady eyes on me and I hurried back indoors.

The day passed incredibly slowly. I thought about weaving a basket to help pass the time, but I couldn't find any dry reeds or grasses in the snow. When it finally got dark, I hurried across the frozen lake to wait for Hawk. He arrived, carrying food and a goatskin.

'How are you?' he said.

'I'm fine,' I replied, hoping he wouldn't hear the hopelessness in my voice. He handed me the food. 'Any news of Moon?'

Hawk shook his head. 'He still hasn't come round.'

It went on like that for seven days. No change in Moon's condition. I often took out the amulet and wished for another dream. But the eyes stayed dull. Perhaps the amulet was punishing me. Or, even worse, it had given up on me altogether.

'I wish Crow was here,' I said to Shadow one afternoon. The sky had turned a dark grey and the crows were all high in the sky, a warning that a storm was coming.

'I know you're good to talk to, Shadow, but only Crow can give me proper advice. What would she do if she felt she'd let someone down?'

Shadow barked softly, as if to say, 'That's easy. She'd stop feeling sorry for herself and try to make up for it. She would help Moon get better.'

'That's great, Shadow,' I said. 'But *how* would she make up for it?'

I pictured Crow stomping around her father's house, thinking. I knew Crow would make a plan. It would be *daring*. It would be *bold*. It would be…

Slowly, a seed for a plan of my own sowed itself in my head. It would mean breaking the rules. It would be dangerous. But it might just work…

That night I discussed the idea with Hawk, begging for his help.

'You've definitely gone mad,' he said, handing me the food. 'No one would dare do that. If we get caught…'

'But the spirits won't let us get caught,' I insisted. 'It's for the good of the village, don't you see? People need Moon back on his feet, looking after the community. And I need to clear my name. Please—'

'Alright,' he said, reluctantly. 'But you'd better

be right about your hunch. Give me time to get to the meadow and move the sheep into the shepherd's hut. I'll meet you outside.'

While Hawk returned to the meadow, I crouched behind the stone and wolfed down some of the food. Hiding the rest in a bush, I thanked the spirits for it and set off in the direction of the village. The storm had passed but it was still raining, making the frozen path slippery.

'No barking now, Shadow,' I warned. 'This is important.'

I had my face hidden inside my fur hood but I knew people would recognise my dog right away if they spotted us.

We slipped past the village to the burial mound where Hawk was already waiting. He helped me move the heavy stone door aside just a crack and I squeezed inside. I hadn't dared bring a light with me, so I stood still for a moment, waiting for my eyes to get used to the dark.

Slowly, the shapes and outlines of skeletons

lying on their wooden pallets formed around me. I picked my way through them until I was standing right in front of the ancient healer. Even in the dark, I could see the sacred spear gleaming in his skeletal hands.

'Please,' I said. 'I have come to borrow your spear. I really need it, not for myself. It's for Moon, the shaman. He has been in a deep sleep for many days and there is no sign he will ever come round. I thought if I could put your spear in his hands, just for a moment, it might help heal him. I'll bring it back as soon as I've finished with it.'

I grasped the spear like I had in Crow's village's burial mound. But this time it wouldn't come away from the healer's grasp. I tugged again and again—it still refused to move.

'Please—' I begged.

Just then I felt the same invisible power I'd felt in Crow's burial mound running from the spear up my arms. It flooded through me. The dark walls

around me vanished and instead there was a bright, starry night sky. As I watched, someone came hobbling towards me. His face was hidden inside a furry hood but a full moon shone above him and I knew he was my friend, the shaman. The ground started to shake all around him and enormous standing stones rose out of the earth to form a towering circle. They all bent towards him, blotting out the stars, and they were all whispering strange words I couldn't understand—

'Are you finished? Come on out, Wolf,' Hawk hissed from the entrance. 'Hurry up before someone sees us.'

A moment later the picture faded and I found myself in the dark again.

Chapter 9
The Whispering Stones

Ten whole days went by after I'd broken into the burial mound but I still had no idea what the message from the spear meant. I had clearly seen a man representing Moon. But what were those strange, towering stones, and why or *what* were they whispering?

Shadow, squatting beside me in the hut, growled.

'Hawk?' I called.

My brother appeared in the doorway. He was not alone. Moon was with him. Happiness flooded through me as I scrambled to my feet. The shaman had come round at last.

'You have a visitor,' joked Hawk.

'Greetings,' said Moon. 'May I come in?'

'Of course.' I made a pile of furs for the shaman to sit on. 'I'm so sorry I didn't warn you about the poison. I thought the seeing-dream was about my brother. But I see now, it was really about you.'

'There is no need to apologise,' said Moon, as I helped him down on the furs and took his stick. He was extremely frail and his cheekbones showed through his papery skin. His eyes were bloodshot. 'I told you before. Seeing-dreams are very difficult to understand. It might take you years before you can read them correctly. The fault was all mine. We keep Wolfsbane in the house to use as poison for our arrow tips. I must have used it by mistake instead of the colouring dye on your bowl. My eyes are not what they used to be. It is I who should apologise for all the trouble I've caused you.'

I knew, of course, that Moon was just trying to

make me feel better. The poison in the bowl might have been just an accident, but I could have saved him from a brush with death if only I hadn't been too hasty about the seeing-dream.

'Moon actually woke up from his deep sleep two days ago,' said Hawk. 'He tried to clear your name the moment he could talk but the villagers will have none of it. They know Moon is your friend and they suspect he is not telling them the truth. They still believe you tried to poison him and they're scared you might try to poison someone else.'

I knew why people thought this, of course. Rain was still doing his best to spread lies about me. I couldn't say that to Moon, of course. No one should speak ill of a child to his father.

'Don't worry too much. The village will soon find something else to be angry about,' said Moon. 'Then you can come home. Meanwhile, I thought I could visit once in a while and teach you how to make healing potions.'

'Like the one Moss made with mustard seeds,' I said. 'The one that saved your life.'

'You helped save my life too,' said Moon. 'And I am grateful for it.'

I looked from Moon to Hawk, unsure if I should say what I wanted to say. In the end, I took the plunge.

'I have to confess, I did something I shouldn't have,' I said. 'I tried to get the sacred spear to put in your hands. I thought its healing power might help make you better. The ancient healer did not allow me to take the spear, but when I touched it I had a vision, just like I had in Crow's burial mound.'

Moon leaned forward. 'What did you see?'

'I saw a man with a moon above his head. I could not see his face because he was wearing a hood but I think he was you. He was surrounded by gigantic standing stones, which bent towards him and whispered strange words.'

Moon's eyes sparkled. 'The Whispering

Stones,' he cried.

'You know what they are?'

'Of course. They are standing stones, enormous boulders carved out of rock and placed to point like giant fingers at the sky. People build sanctuaries with such stones. They have healing powers. The most famous ones are said to whisper secrets to anyone who stands close by them.'

'They sound very mysterious,' I said. 'Are they at the other end of the world?'

'The world is a vast place,' replied Moon. 'Who knows if it is even possible to journey from one end to the other? Nay, I think the standing stones are not at the far end of the world but they are a long way away from Great Island still.'

Moon was quiet for a while. 'I may have woken up from my deep sleep,' he said at last, 'and I can walk with the help of a stick. But I feel I am not yet well. Your vision is no doubt urging me to take the long journey to the Whispering Stones. I always wanted to see them as a child, for many of my shaman friends have travelled to their special sanctuary. It seems now it is my turn to go. There, I shall be healed completely.'

I jumped to my feet, nearly banging my head on the low roof of the hut. Here was a chance for me to right the wrong I had done Moon. 'If my parents let me, I shall come with you,' I said. 'I shall be your servant and your companion. I will cook your food, clean your clothes and you can lean on my shoulder when your feet get tired.'

'That is a good idea,' said Hawk. 'But won't Rain want to go with his father?'

'Rain will have to stay behind to look after the house and the animals,' replied Moon. 'This is not his journey. He was born to be a hunter and a farmer. No, Wolf shall be the one to come with me.'

'Then I'm sure Father will agree that Wolf must go,' said Hawk. 'The time away from the village will give our people time to calm down. And when you come back perfectly strong and

healthy again, they will see how wrong they were about my little brother.' He grinned at me. 'You stay here, Wolf. Moon and I will go and speak to Mother and Father at once.'

Chapter 10
Mysterious Figures on the Shore

It took Moon two days to prepare for the journey. I nearly went mad waiting but on the third night Hawk brought good news.

'I know you're impatient to leave,' he said, 'but Moon's had to find someone to take his place while he's gone. The new shaman will divide his time between our village and his, closer to the shore. Moon's also had to find a farmer to look after his cow and pigs. I guess he doesn't trust Rain to do the job properly. But now everything's prepared and the stars have shown him tonight is the best time to start on your journey.'

I jumped to my feet. 'Tonight? You mean we're

leaving right now?'

Hawk nodded. 'Moon's waiting for you in our shepherd's hut. He's told no one you're going with him, of course. Come on.'

I walked away from my smelly hiding place without once looking back. Father and Mother were standing with Moon outside the shepherd's hut. There was no room for all of them inside. The shaman was wrapped up to his eyes in thick furs, and he carried his stick. I ran into Mother's arms.

'I've packed you some spare furs, and there's dried meat for the journey,' she said, hugging me tight. 'Your spare flint knife is in there too, and some flints so you can make a fire. Take care of yourself and of Moon. You shall be in our thoughts until the day you come back.'

My father placed a hand on my shoulder, a sign of blessing on our island. 'Remember, you come from a long line of brave hunters and farmers. Face any danger you meet on the journey with courage. And obey the shaman's every word. He will be your father in my place while you're away from home.'

'I'll be back before you know it,' I said. 'Remember, this is not my first time away from Great Island after all.'

'Yes,' agreed the shaman, through his furs, 'if we meet no obstacles on the road, we shall be back before next winter sets in.' He looked at Mother. 'You have nothing to worry about, Coral. I promise to bring your son home safely. Come, Wolf.'

We slipped away from the hut without any more fuss. As we skirted our way round the sleeping village and past Moon's house, I was dreading Rain coming out and causing a scene. But the door remained shut. Perhaps Rain was sulking, or had refused to bid his father goodbye.

'Do not judge him too harshly,' said Moon, seeing me look back at the house. 'He made me a special amulet from fish bones. It will protect me from drowning should we have an accident.'

Hawk, who had come with us down to the shore, pointed to a skiff moored to a large rock.

'I bartered for it with a fisherman,' he said. 'It was the strongest boat I could find.'

'Hawk,' I gasped, touched that my brother would give away his precious things to help me. 'Thank you very much. And look, it's lined with fur to keep us warm, and there's an oar too.'

I made to step into it but Moon pulled me gently back. 'We need to ask the spirits for their protection first.' He reached into his bag to draw out a large seashell. He placed it at the foot of the rock the skiff was moored to.

'We ask the spirits to guard this shell until we come back to claim it,' he said.

'And I leave this flint stone alongside it,' I said, digging into my own bag. 'May the spirits guide us home safely to find it again.'

Moon piled sand onto our offerings to hide them while I stepped onto the skiff, making it rock.

'Come on, Shadow,' I said. 'Get aboard.'

Shadow remained stubbornly onshore. Our last adventure at sea, when we both nearly drowned, was obviously still fresh in his mind. He growled at the water.

'Courage,' I said, stepping back onshore to scoop him up in my arms. 'If we get caught in a storm again, we both know we only have to keep afloat until we end up on land.'

The sun was just about to come up as, at last, Hawk waded into the water to push the skiff away from the shore. We said our goodbyes and set out to sea. After so many storms, it was going to be a clear day. The world glowed with a pink light so intense, it hurt my eyes. The gulls in the rocks squawked.

I felt a ripple of excitement as Hawk grew smaller in the distance. My first adventure on the sea had led me to Seal Island, and to Crow and Sparrow. I wondered where this one would take me.

I turned to the rising sun and sang my Wolf Song as I paddled. On the shore, wolves appeared among the jagged rocks and joined in with me.

'Ah,' said the shaman, closing his eyes. 'It is

very special magic when wolves howl during the day. They have come to wish us good luck.'

Once I'd sung my song, I turned back to take one last look at Great Island. Hawk was gone and there was no sign of the wolves. But among the rocks, I could see figures draped in furry cloaks. They seemed to be doing a wild dance, shaking their fists above their heads. One of them hurled something into the sea, an offering no doubt.

Clutching my dream-amulet without even knowing, I wondered who they might be.

Chapter 11
The Start of the Journey

'Look,' I said. 'There's someone on the shore.'

Moon looked up but the leaping figures were no longer there. 'It was probably someone looking for auk eggs,' he said.

'I saw them throwing something into the sea.'

'They could be fisherman then,' said the shaman. 'I always tell them to throw offerings of food into the waves.'

I settled back on my seat and continued paddling. My arms were already hurting but I was glad I remembered exactly how to paddle. 'Do you know the way to the Whispering Stones?' I asked Moon.

'The shamans who travelled there talked in great detail of their journey. If I remember correctly, we sail first to Seal Island, as you did. From there we cross on to a land so big, it is said you can fit a thousand Great Islands in it. Then we travel south on foot, always keeping the Unmoving Star behind us.'

I paddled on, stopping only once in a while to rest my weary arms. Every now and then, Shadow would growl at the shore. But every time I looked, there was nothing there except gulls sitting on boulders or the occasional stunted tree. Perhaps my trusted dog was still nervous about the sea and wanted to get back onto dry land.

The skiff carried us down to the very tip of Great Island. From there, we struck out towards Seal Island. Even though it was getting dark, I could see its dark peaks rising against the skies and I wished we had time to stop and visit Crow. We could visit Sparrow too. His own island was also nearby. I'd tell both my friends about the dream-amulet, and the new vision the sacred spear had sent me.

The sun had almost set in a fiery red sky, when Shadow started barking and pawing at the furs lining the boat.

'What's the matter?' I asked.

Shadow whined and spun round in a panic. A wet patch had appeared in the furs.

'I think we're taking in water,' I gasped at Moon. 'I don't know how, but the boat has sprung a leak.'

Moon, who'd been sleeping at the prow, opened his eyes and stared at the wet patch. It was growing bigger by the moment.

'I'll plug it up with one of my spare furs,' I said, putting down the oar and struggling to open my hunting bag.

'I fear that won't save us,' said Moon calmly. 'We'll have to try and get to Seal Island. We'll repair the skiff there.'

I shifted my weight so that the skiff changed

direction and paddled as hard as I could. Shadow barked and, to my horror, leapt over the side.

'Shadow!' I called, knowing how much he hated the sea and fearing the worst.

My dog ignored me and started paddling towards Seal Island. I rowed after him, even though I knew the sinking skiff could never catch up with him. From the corner of my eye, I caught movement in the water. My heart sank. Sharks were circling the skiff.

Moon saw them too and started chanting a spell to make them go away. I threw one of my arrowheads into the waves as sacrifice.

'Please,' I begged the spirits, 'make these dangerous creatures disappear.'

The sharks only swooped closer to the skiff, until I was terrified their fins would actually rip through the fur and wood. I have no idea how long I stared in horror at the sea but at last Moon nudged me.

'Wolf, look.'

Flickering torches were flickering across the water and a voice called out. 'Hold on, out there! We are coming for you.'

I saw a large skiff approaching. There were two men in it, both rowing. Expertly, they pulled up alongside us until one of them could reach out and haul Moon to safety. The other one reached out for me.

I had barely landed in the large skiff when ours disappeared completely underwater. The sharks dived after it.

'I can't thank you enough,' I said to the two men. 'Those sharks would have had us if you hadn't come along.'

'Your dog alerted us to your plight,' said one of the men. 'He's a real hero. You're lucky you were so close to shore. We're fishermen and we were getting ready to sail when he scrambled onto the beach, barking his head off.'

More torches flickered on the shore as the men guided the skiff onto the sand. A crowd had gathered and children were pointing at Moon and I eagerly.

A dog barked joyfully. 'Shadow,' I said. 'Where are you, boy?'

My dog came forward, his tail wagging furiously. He was followed by a tall girl holding a spear. 'Wolf, how exciting to see you again! Welcome back to Seal Island.'

It was Crow!

Chapter 12
Seal Island

Crow called orders at the other people on the beach. 'Get that old man out of those wet furs and into dry ones. Hurry up or the chill will kill him. And bring hot drinks. Both the old man and the boy need to warm their insides.'

Crow turned and grinned at me as I peeled off the wet furs to get into the ones her people had brought. She had grown even taller since I'd last seen her. Her wavy hair was wilder too.

'That old man, as you've called him, is Moon, my shaman,' I explained. 'He's not well and we were travelling to another land to seek the help of the Whispering Stones. But our skiff started taking in water and sank.'

'This sounds like quite a tale! You can tell me all about it when we're indoors,' said Crow. 'There's plenty of stew left. Come—'

Seated round the fire in her house, a contented Shadow beside me, I told Crow my story, beginning with the day the ancient healer gave me the dream-amulet to the horrific moment our skiff sank.

'To be honest, I find it very suspicious how your skiff suddenly started taking in water,' Crow interrupted my story. 'It sounds like you were in deep water. You could not have grazed the bottom against a rock. I think someone must have tampered with it before you set out. It's possible to make a slight crack in a skiff that will slowly get bigger under pressure from the sea. Perhaps somebody actually wanted your boat to sink in the middle of the ocean.'

I thought of the hooded figures dancing wildly on the shore and wondered if one of them might have tampered with our skiff. It was a chilling thought. Who could possibly want me and Moon to drown?

'I shall get my people to build you a new and stronger skiff,' said Crow. She gestured at Moon, who was falling asleep by the fire. Even though he was dry and warm, he was still trembling.

'I hate the idea of you travelling on your own. You need someone to help you look after the old shaman. A strong hunter and explorer, like me. I'm coming to the Whispering Stones with you.'

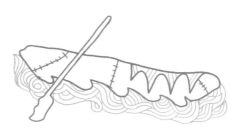

Chapter 13
Forests and Mountains

It took only a few days to build a new skiff and make it watertight. Once it was loaded with supplies—Crow's father would not let us leave without enough food to last us at least a moon cycle—we thanked everyone, offered a new sacrifice at the water's edge and resumed our journey.

With two young people paddling, the going was much easier, and quicker. We passed a few small islands. Some had villages nestled among the rocks, others seemed to be completely uninhabited. We stopped on one of these one evening, to spend a night out of the skiff.

Although we'd had good weather, Moon had shivered with cold all day and I wanted him to sleep somewhere warm and dry.

'Somebody's been here before us, and recently,' said Crow, while we hauled the skiff onto dry land. She pointed to some large footprints in the earth. 'Boots, different sizes too. There's been more than one person here.'

Shadow sniffed at the footprints and growled fiercely.

'Don't you like the people who made them?' I asked. 'Perhaps they were hungry people who came in a boat from a nearby island looking for auk eggs. There are a lot of auks here.'

While Crow made a fire, Shadow and I went off in search of eggs for a treat. I was getting tired of dried meat. We returned with three enormous ones, which I poked into the crackling firewood. Moon thanked the spirits before we wolfed them down. Rowing all day had given me a huge appetite.

Afterwards, we spread our furs under a tree and went to sleep, Shadow curled up beside me. Once or twice, I heard Moon coughing. I was starting to get worried about him. Would he be able to make it all the way to the Whispering Stones?

In the morning, I woke up to find Crow standing

by the skiff, which she had just dragged back to the water's edge. She was looking at something in the palm of her hand.

'What have you found?' I asked. 'An interesting looking pebble?'

She didn't reply but put the object inside her tunic and looked out to sea. 'It's going to be another clear day,' she said. 'Let's get going as soon as we can.'

Once again, we made good progress and by nightfall, we beached the skiff at a sandy shore backed with high, white cliffs.

'This is not another island,' said Moon excitedly. 'This is the Land of the Whispering Stones. From now on, we travel on foot. But let us thank the spirits first, and ask for their help with the rest of our journey. Who knows what challenges lie ahead? And we must rest.'

Crow went off to hunt and came back with a hare. We cooked it and washed it down with water from a nearby spring. Then Crow and I found a cave at the base of the cliffs. We dragged the skiff into it and piled mountains of seaweed on top of it.

'I beg the spirits to protect it so no one finds it,' I said. 'Hopefully, it will still be here when we come back.'

Shadow kept running up and down the shore, sniffing at tufts of grass and growling.

'What's the matter with him?' I wondered aloud. 'He's going to wake Moon.'

'He keeps sniffing things he doesn't like,' said Crow, and I noticed that her hand slipped inside her tunic where she'd put the mysterious pebble. I didn't ask her about it. I knew she would talk about it when she was ready.

'I am so glad you decided to come with us,' I said. 'I only wish Sparrow was here too. I miss him.'

'Sparrow often visits Seal Island to tell me stories about his hunts for deer and rabbits,' replied Crow. 'If his tales are true, he's becoming a great hunter in his own right. If you remember, his island is close to mine. We must visit him when we get back to Seal Island.'

In the morning, we thanked the spirits for getting us across the sea safely then started on our journey again.

'We must always keep the sea to our left,' said Moon. 'At night, the Unmoving Star should be directly behind us.'

I walked with my eyes and ears wide open. Everything around me was so different from the island I considered my home. The colour of the soil was darker, the green of the leaves brighter, the scent of sap in the air stronger. I had never seen so many trees packed close together before.

In some places, their branches met overhead and cast a day-long shadow on the ground. I could hear wild noises coming from the bushes and I shuddered to think what kind of wild creatures made them. Crow had no such fears. She disappeared among the trees often and always came back unharmed, and with something for the pot.

We walked for days on end, resting often to give Moon time to regain his strength. As we moved further south, we saw people clearing land for farming. Some ignored us as we passed by but most glared suspiciously. Only Shadow, who took great pleasure in sniffing and licking their hands, made them smile.

Early one morning, Moon was talking to me and Crow about the stars when he stumbled over a root. He winced in pain.

'Are you alright?' I asked.

Moon's face was pinched as he slowly lifted his foot off the ground.

'I think I've twisted my ankle.'

'Let's stop for a rest,' I said. 'I'll bathe your ankle. It'll be better in no time.'

But, when I removed Moon's boots, I saw right away that his leg and foot were red and swollen, and he had awful blisters. They looked really painful and some of them had burst.

'Don't make a fuss,' said Moon, as if reading my mind. 'They don't really hurt, and they will be healed along with everything else once we reach the Whispering Stones.'

Chapter 14
Stones from a Sling!

We walked slower that day. I was worried Moon might never make it as far as the Whispering Stones. It wasn't just his swollen ankle and the blisters that worried me. He seemed to be getting thinner and weaker by the day, no matter how much Crow and I fed him. I wondered if there was still poison left inside him, slowly killing him.

'How much longer before we reach the Whispering Stones?' I asked one morning.

'We have been walking for forty-one days,' said Crow. 'I have kept a tally with notches on my spear.'

Moon, who had overheard the conversation, spoke up. 'I would say we have another forty to go.'

That was bad news. Moon would never survive another forty days on the road, even if the weather was getting warmer as we travelled south. I racked my brain to find a solution, even taking the dream-amulet out and begging it for help.

In the afternoon, we came to a small village on the banks of the river. We exchanged more arrowheads for food and the villagers made us most welcome. The children all came out to play with Shadow, who chased them playfully.

'We should stop here for a few days,' I insisted. 'We all need a proper rest, and time for Moon's ankle to heal.'

Moon started to protest but Crow stepped in. 'We're not taking another step until you are better,' she said firmly. 'Your leg is slowing us down. Once it's healed, we can walk faster and make up for lost time.'

One of the villagers, a farmer called Sickle, offered us the use of a large storehouse. It was built of solid stone, with wooden hooks on the walls where Sickle hung her tools. At this time of year, there was not much stored in it. All the grain collected at harvest time had been eaten or bartered.

'You can stay here for as long as you like,' she said. 'All I ask is that you children help me in the field. It is the time to break up the soil, ready for sowing after the harsh winter. It'll be nice to have someone to talk to. I'm a childless widow and alone most of the time.'

'I'll go out hunting to get something for the pot too,' said Crow.

Sickle seemed very pleased with that idea. 'It's a deal then,' she said.

The rest of the village turned out to have a good stare as we made our way to the fields. Most of the people were dressed in clean deerskins and carried spears or tools very much like ours back on Great Island. Once Sickle had explained who we were, they returned to their jobs.

Still, I couldn't shake the feeling that some of them were still watching us. Every now and then I'd look up from the plough and spot someone staring from behind a bush. But I was determined not to take any notice. A stranger back home would be stared at too.

A few days passed, but Moon's ankle refused to heal. The swelling was still as big as ever. His breathing came in rasps and he coughed every time he tried to speak.

'I'll get some fresh water and wash your feet,' I said, trying not to sound too worried. 'I noticed a stream outside the village.'

Picking up a goatskin, I made my way out of the storehouse. Shadow trotted at my heels, sniffing at every stone we passed. It was getting dark and the air was cold with the promise of night-frost. As I was bending down to fill the skin, Shadow growled and barked. I heard a whizzing noise and a stone flew right over my head. It hit a tree trunk behind me.

'Hey!' I called. 'Watch it!'

There was a blur of deerskin in the bushes and I caught a glimpse of someone ducking. Shadow leapt into the stream, barking angrily, but soon dashed back out as the water sloshed around his legs.

Another stone came flying, this one from behind me. It hit me right in the small of my back.

'Ouch!' I cried.

Thankfully, a moment later, Crow stepped out from the trees. 'Are you alright, Wolf?'

'Some of the village children are throwing stones,' I said, rubbing my back.

She glared around. 'Go home, you lot.'

Shadow growled to show he agreed with her.

There was no reply from the bushes, only the snapping of twigs as the cuplrits ran away. Crow and I filled the goatskin.

'It's a good job you were following me,' I said. 'Those children could have knocked me out.'

'Those children need a good talking to,' hissed Crow. 'Come on, let's get back. But let's not tell Moon anything about this. He has enough to worry about.'

In the storehouse, Moon was sat near the fire. He was talking to Sickle. An older man in patchy deerskin sat with them.

'I have been talking to Sickle about our journey,' said Moon, smiling happily. 'It turns out we don't need to walk all the way to the

Whispering Stones after all. We can go by river. This man here, Cloud, will take us in his boat. He's Sickle's cousin. I shall pay him with a necklace of green beads from my bag.'

The man in the patchy deerskins nodded to show he agreed. It seemed he couldn't speak. He used his hands to make signs and words but Crow and I could not understand any of them. When he saw our blank expressions, he nodded at Sickle who explained on his behalf. 'Cloud says there is a wide river that will take you directly to the place of the Whispering Stones. But it's not safe to navigate its fast-flowing waters. Sickle will take you along the gentler streams that feed off of it. Even so, that will cut at least ten days off your journey.'

Cloud nodded to show that Sickle had explained everything correctly.

'That's very good news indeed,' coughed Moon. 'We leave tomorrow at dawn.'

After the meal, we stretched our furs on the

floor. 'We need to close the storehouse securely,' whispered Crow. 'I'm sure we're being followed.'

I looked around me in alarm. 'By who?'

Crow reached inside her furs and drew out a small object. It was an arrowhead.

'Is that what you found on that deserted island where we stopped to rest? I assumed it was a pebble.'

Crow nodded. 'How did it get to the deserted island, I wonder?'

'I have had the feeling that someone's been watching us,' I said.

'You too?' said Crow.

'It must be people from the various settlements we passed,' cut in Moon who'd overheard the conversation. 'Most of them would have never seen a stranger before. They'd be very suspicious, scared even.' He snuggled into his furs. 'Now let's get some sleep.'

Chapter 15
River Journey

The river journey took us along streams with thick grass and flowers on the banks. There seemed to be bees and butterflies everywhere.

At night, we moored to make a fire and cook supper, although Moon always remained on the skiff. Shadow took to sleeping beside him, his head resting on the old man's chest. Perhaps he could sense that Moon was sick and wanted to protect him.

Cloud had a bone pipe, which he played after each meal. His music was soft and spellbinding, and it made me think of safe things, like home and my parents, and my own bed. Crow and I made more arrowheads for bartering. We soon had a small pile.

Twenty notches on Crow's spear later, we came to the end of our river journey. Moon paid Cloud and he touched his lips with bunched fingers to say 'thank you.'

As Crow and I helped Moon onto the bank, I spotted a village. It was the largest collection of buildings I had ever seen. Our houses on Great Island are half-sunk in earth to help keep them warm but these homes stood proud on flat ground. They were well-built, with clean white walls and thatch on the sloping roofs. The pathways were teeming with busy people carrying baskets and pots.

A man appeared in a doorway. He was a small fellow, with stooping shoulders and missing teeth but he had a cheerful smile.

'Greetings, travellers,' he said. 'Have you come far? Do you seek the Place of the Living?'

'We seek the Whispering Stones,' I replied,

holding on to Shadow who was trying to chew the man's boots.

'Your old friend looks tired,' said the man with missing teeth. 'Come inside and have something to eat. My wife makes a nice barley porridge.'

'We have not much left to give in return,' said Moon. 'Just a few arrowheads my friends here have just made. Although they're very good ones. People on our islands far north are expert craftsmen when it comes to making flint weapons.'

The man smiled at Moon. 'I can see by the amulets around your neck that you are a shaman. I wanted to become one too when I was a child but sadly I did not have the gift. My name is Sky, by the way, on account of the fact that I was always peering up at the heavens when I was a baby.'

As we sat around the fire, eating thick, creamy porridge, Moon said, 'You asked if we are looking for the Place of the Living…'

'That's right,' explained Sky. 'Please do not be

offended, but I couldn't help noticing that you walk with a bad limp and that your eyes are cloudy. I see these signs in many people who are in need of healing. And many of those come here to visit the Place of the Living. There is a circle of standing timbers there where healing ceremonies are held. It is said the ancient timbers heal anyone who dances around them.'

Sky's wife, a round woman with twinkly eyes who was called Earth, dished out more porridge. 'Ha! Or it might be the food and the expensive potions that they feed the sick that do the healing. I believe a great slab of meat and a drink made with the right herbs will heal any sickness.'

'But the world of the spirits is indeed a mystery,' said Sky, smiling at his wife's words. 'You have come at the right time too, strangers. The stars are aligned tonight. There will be a ceremony.'

'And what of the Whispering Stones?' I asked. 'Are they in the Place of the Living?'

'Not quite,' replied Sky. 'You have reached a vast sanctuary. It is divided into two parts, the Place of the Living where people come to be healed, and the Place of the Dead where important people are buried. They are buried there because it's a place where the spirits dwell. The very ground is full of their mysterious power. You will find the Whispering Stones in the Place of the Dead.

I thought of my vision. I had seen Moon at the Whispering Stones. Now I realised that they were in the Place of the Dead. But he needed to go to the Place of the Living, to be healed. So what did my vision mean? It was very confusing.

'I am not important enough to be allowed inside the sanctuary,' said Sky, interrupting my thoughts. 'But you can see the Whispering Stones from outside. They stand in two circles, one inside the other. Enormous, they are. It is said the Whispering Stones hold many secret powers. If you put your ear to them you can hear the voices

of the spirits.'

I wondered what the stones would whisper to me if I put my ear to them. Would they reveal a secret, or my future?

Suddenly there was a scuffling noise outside the door. Shadow growled deep in his throat and Crow dashed outside, leaving the rest of us looking from one to the other.

'It's no one,' she said when she came back.

'It is good you are so vigilant,' said Sky. 'Sadly, a place like the Whispering Stones attracts a lot of thieves. Keep your wits about you when you're outside.'

'How long do you plan to stay in the village?' asked Earth.

'Probably a few days,' said Moon.

Earth smiled. 'You can lodge here if you want. Your arrowheads will make for good bartering.'

'That is most kind of you, thank you,' said Moon. He turned to Sky. 'How do I get into the Place of the Living for the healing ceremony?'

'Yes,' I added. 'We want to get close to the Whispering Stones.'

Sky looked from Moon to me. 'You cannot get into the Place of the Dead without first taking part in the healing ceremony in the Place of the Living. It is surrounded by a deep ditch guarded day and night by apprentice shamans. Those seeking healing are transported from one place to another along the sacred river. Children are not usually allowed in but I think you can claim your shaman needs help with walking.'

'But what about Crow?' I asked.

'I'd rather not come,' said Crow quickly. 'Hunting is more my thing than attending sacred ceremonies.'

'But how do I get in?' asked Moon.

'You will have to pay the men in charge,' said Sky. 'Shamans, like you. A freshly killed deer, or a fat sheep heavy with lambs will secure you a place in the ceremony tonight. Failing that, you could try bribing one of the guards with a well-made tool or pot. It doesn't always work, mind.'

Moon coughed and wiped his mouth with a furry rag. To my horror, I could see blood on it.

Crow leapt to her feet. 'I think I heard that noise at the door again,' she said. 'Wolf, come with me.'

We both rushed outside. 'But there's no one here,' I said, looking round.

'I know,' said Crow. 'I just wanted to get you out here. Did you see that Moon coughed up blood?'

'I did, he's getting worse.' I couldn't hide my concern. We could both see that Moon's time was running out.

'We have to make sure he gets get into the healing ceremony *tonight*. Come on, I have an idea.'

I followed Crow along a narrow street until we came to a small group of women chatting outside a house.

'Where is the market, please?' asked Crow.

'Keep going to the end of this path,' answered one of the women. 'Then turn right and you will find a meeting place. That's where we hold the daily market.'

'Thanks,' said Crow. We hurried down the path and soon found ourselves in a busy area where people were bartering goods. Most of them looked like me, pale and with reddish hair but a few were darker skinned. Their eyes too were dark and they spoke a language I did not understand.

I was drawn to them immediately. Who knew which part of the world they had come from, what stories they could tell?

Crow held up her spear.

'Who will trade a sheep for this spear?' she called. 'A very special spear that has brought down many a deer and wild boar. It is imbued with their power.'

I was amazed that Crow wanted to part with her spear. It was her most treasured possession. The notches on its shaft told so much about her life—the number of animals she'd caught, the number of days she'd spent on her travels. And yet she would give it up for Moon.

'Ha!' said a passer-by. 'A spear for a sheep? That's not much of a barter.'

As more people turned up their nose at the spear, I knew I had to do something. If we couldn't get Moon into the healing ceremony tonight, it might be too late. This was a desperate situation. Gritting my teeth, I whipped out the dream amulet.

'It's not just a spear we're bartering,' I said. 'We have a powerful amulet too. Used by an ancient healer in a village far away. Come on, people. Two special items for the price of one sheep.'

A fat man with curly red hair stepped forward. 'Can I have a look at the offered goods?'

Crow and I jumped at the chance before the man could change his mind. We held out the spear and the amulet. 'This is very good work,' he said, inspecting the spear and the amulet. 'I have a spare sheep to barter. She is getting old but she's still a fine animal.' He turned to a younger man, also with curly red hair. 'Son, bring the eldest sheep.'

The sheep was dragged forward and I watched sadly as the man hung the dream amulet around his neck. The glazed eyes seemed to stare at me accusingly.

A tidal wave of guilt and fear washed over me. Had I put my future as a shaman at risk? Would the ancient healer be angry with me for giving away his gift? Had I done the right thing? My head was swirling with confusion as Crow and I led the sheep to Sky's house. Moon was lying by the fire, his eyes closed and his hands laid across his bony chest.

'He has been coughing more blood,' said Earth solemnly. 'I have given him a soothing potion but you need to get him into the healing ceremony, tonight.'

Looking at Moon, I knew I had done the right thing. His life was more important to me than anything else in the world.

Chapter 16
The Place of the Living

Late in the evening, a thick mist rose and wrapped itself around the village. Leaving Earth to look after Shadow, we walked slowly through it, Moon leaning on me and Crow dragging the sheep. The poor, bleating creature did indeed gain us entry to the sanctuary and I hoped its new owners would treat it kindly.

'Good luck. I'll see you back at Sky's,' said Crow. She disappeared into the crowd. Moon and I followed the other pilgrims through a wide doorway cut in a high, circular earth bank. Before us lay the strangest sight I had ever seen. Circle within circle of tall wooden posts stood before me, all pointing up to the sky like giant fingers. I saw an enormous stone at the centre of the smallest circle. A great fire was burning on it and there was a smell of cooking meat.

'What is that?' I asked Moon.

'I believe it is a feasting stone,' he coughed. 'There's a cow roasting on it. They are preparing the great feast.'

'It must be the healing meal Earth mentioned,' I said.

A thick-set shaman with a flowing beard and a stick in each hand approached the stone and held the sticks up to the skies. The mist made him look blurry, like something seen through water.

'I am Midnight,' he called. 'I have been entrusted by the spirits to lead you through your healing journey. Gather round, all who came to be healed.'

Moon let go of my shoulder and held up his hand to show that he wanted to approach the feasting stone without my help. He shuffled through the sacred circles with the rest of the crowd.

'These wooden pillars around us are made from the trunks of sacred trees,' said Midnight. 'They connect the earth with the skies, drawing on their hidden powers to heal all who come to seek their help. Let us dance around them to draw on their power.'

Midnight put down his sticks and one of his assistants handed him a bone flute. He started playing and those who wanted to be healed joined hands to form a line. They danced around the great stone, in and out among the pillars. Moon stumbled along with them, chanting along to the eerie music.

The dancing went on until almost sunrise and I marvelled at how such frail men could keep going for so long. The power of the wooden

pillars was no doubt
already having an effect on them.

By now, the cow on the feasting stone had roasted
to perfection. Midnight held up his hands to stop
the dancing.

'It is time for the feast!' he shouted. 'Let us eat
and drink in honour of the spirits.'

The men fell on the meat like a pack of wolves,
tearing at the flesh with bare hands. Assistants
rushed round with bowls of water and the men
drank deep.

Moon came up to me with a wild look in his
eyes. 'I can feel the sickness starting to leave my
body already. I shall be completely healed, I tell
you. Healed!'

'The sun is nearly up,' called Midnight. 'Let us
go to the Place of the Dead and say thank you to
their spirits.'

Chapter 17
The Place of the Dead

We followed Midnight to the banks of a river where a line of skiffs lay waiting. We boarded them in silence, four people to a skiff. I felt goosebumps on my arms as I paddled closer to the Place of the Dead. At last I would be able to see the sacred Whispering Stones.

Docking at a grassy bank, we formed a double line and made our way across a perfectly straight pathway to another round earth-bank. We passed through another wide doorway and there, rising through the mist, stood the Whispering Stones.

I shall never forget that moment. It was awe-inspiring. The Whispering Stones looked exactly like they had in my vision: a gigantic circle of standing boulders with a stone crown on top. They glowed a shimmering red in the morning light, as if there was fire inside them.

'Behold,' said Midnight, and I noticed that he was standing inside a second circle of stones. 'Come forward, all you who have been healed. This morning we dance to celebrate the ones who have gone before us, the ones who are now part of the earth and the sky. Their spirits make the world richer for us all.'

As Moon joined the others inside the second circle, I found myself alone again. I looked at the nearest stone. Perhaps it was just my imagination, but I could feel a power coming out of it, drawing me closer.

As if in a dream, I moved up to it and placed the palm of my right hand against it. At once, I could hear whispering voices and a jumble of images raced in front of my eyes.

I saw myself holding the dream-amulet.

Find that which you have so nobly given away, whispered the stones. *It is the key to your future. Find the dream-amulet again...*

Now the voices seemed to be floating at me from all the other stones, swarming around me like invisible bees.

Find the dream-amulet. It is the key to your future...

And then the pictures showed me growing taller, becoming a man. The amulet in my hand was swinging backwards and forwards. The eyes were blazing.

The voices continued to whisper. *Remember, it is not by beating your chest for past mistakes that you move forward. It is by accepting that everyone fails sometimes. Learn from your mistakes and face the future with humility and courage.*

'Yes!' I shouted back. 'I will—' And then I caught sight of Moon—the real person, not someone in the stones' pictures—stumbling towards me. His eyes were wide with horror and he was pointing a trembling finger at something, or someone, behind me.

'Wolf, watch out,' screamed Moon. He lunged forward and pulled me roughly aside. A moment later one of the Whispering Stones came crashing down.

Even as I fell to the grass, I caught a glimpse of several people standing where the stone had been. They were only there for a moment—then they ran away—but I recognised one of them immediately. He had my amulet dangling round his neck.

It was Rain!

Chapter 18
A New Adventure

'Rain… my own son tried to kill you,' said Moon.

Even though I'd been brought back to the safety of Sky's house, I was still shaking. Sky and Earth looked at me anxiously. Shadow nuzzled my arm. Crow stood glowering at the door. She'd made a replacement spear by sharpening a stick.

'Someone actually tried to kill him?' said Earth.

Moon nodded gravely and I could see tears running down his cheeks. 'I wouldn't have believed it if I hadn't seen him with my own eyes. He followed us all the way here with his friends. I was twirling round in the dance and I spotted them pushing the stone over.'

'I think Rain has tried to kill Wolf more than once,' announced Crow. 'I bet he put the poison in the bowl Moon used in the wolf ceremony. It was intended for *Wolf.* He had no idea his father would use the bowl first. And he made the crack in the boat to take in water. He must have hoped that somehow Wolf would drown but his father would survive.'

'Yes,' Moon shuddered and closed his eyes. 'He made a fishbone amulet to protect me.'

'And the figures dancing on the shore of Great Island,' I said. 'Those could have been Rain and his friends too, offering sacrifice for their own journey after us.'

'And those children who shot stones at you by the stream,' added Crow. 'They might have been Rain and his friends too.'

'But why would a child try to kill?' said Sky.

We both looked to Moon for an answer. He stared into the fire before he spoke and I don't think I've ever seen so much sadness in a man's eyes before.

'Sadly, it seems my son will stop at nothing to take Wolf's place as the future shaman. I underestimated the boy. He is much stronger than I thought, but for all the wrong reasons.'

'Where do you think is he now?' asked Earth. 'Do you think he will go back home to your village?'

'I suspect he will not dare face me,' replied Moon. 'Even though, as his father, I would eventually forgive him. Who knows where he will go next? I fear I might have lost my only son forever...'

I got to my feet. 'I shall go after him,' I said. 'I want my amulet back. He must have stolen it off the man with red curly hair. The Whispering Stones told me it is the key to my future.'

Crow's eyes flashed with excitement. 'And I shall come with you, Wolf of Great Island. You will need my help. Who knows were Rain is hiding, or going, and what he will do if you catch up with him?'

'But if you go with Wolf, how will Moon get back to Great Island on his own?' said Sky.

'I shall wait for them here,' replied Moon. 'I promised Wolf's family I would bring him back home safely. I will not return home without him. Besides, there is a lot to keep me occupied here.'

'You have a home here for as long as you need it,' said Earth kindly. 'It will be good to have a shaman under our roof.'

'And I can pay for my keep by making clay bowls,' added Moon. 'I shall also make a new bowl for Wolf to have when he gets back. It is settled then.'

We had river fish for dinner, which Earth and Sky roasted over the fire. It was delicious but I remember Moon ate very little. He often seemed lost, unaware of what the rest of us were saying. I couldn't imagine what pain a parent must feel when they realise that their child has lost his way.

Long after the feast I lay on my furs, thinking. I'd discovered a lot about myself during the visit to the Whispering Stones. I was quick to punish myself and slow to celebrate my gifts and achievements. True, I'd been too confident about reading seeing-dreams. I'd made a big mistake trying to read the first one and ignoring Moon's warnings. But in the end, I had made up for it by bringing Moon to the Place of the Living. My strong side had won over my weaker side.

The words of the Whispering Stones echoed in my head again.

Remember, it is not by beating your chest for past mistakes that you move forward. It is by accepting that everyone fails sometimes. Learn from your mistakes and face the future with humility and courage.

That's what I promised myself to do.

I would find Rain wherever he was, and I would get my amulet back.

There was a loud creak as the door to the hut

opened. Crow came in. She'd gone out hunting after dinner, and I could see she'd caught a hare.

'Wolf,' she whispered. 'Get up. I've just seen Rain. If you want to catch up with him, we have to leave right now.'

She grabbed her bundle, hoisted it to her shoulder and headed out of the hut without once looking back.

I picked up my belongings, indicated to Shadow to follow me and hurried after her into the freezing cold.

It seemed my new adventure was about to start right away…

Wolf's journey will continue in

The
Mysterious
Island

DiSCUSSION POINtS

Wolf's story is full of **adventure** in *The Whispering Stones*.

- What springs to mind when you think of the word 'adventure'? Do you think this would be the same for Wolf, or the other characters in the story?
- How does danger play a role in adventures?
- Which characters seem the most adventurous?

Relationships are at the heart of the story. There are not only connections between Wolf and his friends, his family and his rivals, but also between other characters too.

- How many different relationships appear in *The Whispering Stones*? Are some stronger than others, and why?
- Why are these relationships important? What do

they tell us about the characters?

- Do you think that any relationships will change in the future? Why/why not?

Stonehenge and **Woodhenge** appear in this book as the mysterious Place of the Dead and Place of the Living.

- Why do you think the characters, and Neolithic people, would travel great distances to see these places?

- Archaeologists found that Stonehenge has an entrance that matches the direction of the midsummer sunrise and midwinter sunset, and Woodhenge has an entrance for the opposite. What do you think this tells us about how Neolithic people viewed the seasons and nature?

- Stonehenge would have taken a very long time to build as Neolithic people do not have the same technology as we do, in modern times. How do you think they would have done this?

There are many things Wolf has to **accept** during the story. Some are good, some are confusing, and some are dangerous.

- Which experiences do you think Wolf is willing to accept and why?

- Are there any moments where Wolf has to accept something he was not expecting or something he disagreed with? How does he deal with this?

- Which characters are unwilling to accept the truth? Why do you think they do this?

The Whispering Stones is all about the **choices** people make and the consequences.

- Which choices have the most consequences? Are there any choices that shift other characters' decisions?

- Are there any difficult decisions in the story?

- What do people's choices tell us about their personalities?